# Unicorn Princesses
## MOON'S DANCE

# Unicorn Princesses

## MOON'S DANCE

Emily Bliss

illustrated by Sydney Hanson

BLOOMSBURY
NEW YORK  LONDON  OXFORD  NEW DELHI  SYDNEY

First published in the United States of America in April 2018
by Bloomsbury Children's Books
www.bloomsbury.com

Bloomsbury is a registered trademark of Bloomsbury Publishing Plc

For information about permission to reproduce selections from this book, write to
Permissions, Bloomsbury Children's Books, 1385 Broadway, New York, NY 10018
Bloomsbury books may be purchased for business or promotional use.
For information on bulk purchases please contact Macmillan Corporate and
Premium Sales Department at specialmarkets@macmillan.com

Library of Congress Cataloging-in-Publication Data
Names: Bliss, Emily, author. | Hanson, Sydney, illustrator.
Title: Moon's dance / by Emily Bliss ; illustrated by Sydney Hanson.
Description: New York : Bloomsbury, 2018. | Series: Unicorn princesses ; 6
Summary: Cressida eagerly accepts Princess Moon's invitation to attend the
annual Starlight Ball, but when Ernest the wizard-lizard causes the ballroom to
disappear, the unicorn princesses must magically prepare another space.
Identifiers: LCCN 2017020573 (print) | LCCN 2017036916 (e-book)
ISBN 978-1-68119-652-7 (paperback) • ISBN 978-1-68119-653-4 (hardcover)
ISBN 978-1-68119-654-1 (e-book)
Subjects: | CYAC: Balls (Parties)—Fiction. | Unicorns—Fiction. |
Princesses—Fiction. | Magic—Fiction. | Fantasy.
Classification: LCC PZ7.1.B633 Moo 2018 (print) | LCC PZ7.1.B633 (e-book) |
DDC [Fic]—dc23
LC record available at https://lccn.loc.gov/2017020573

Book design by Jessie Gang and John Candell
Typeset by Westchester Publishing Services
Printed and bound in the U.S.A. by Berryville Graphics Inc., Berryville, Virginia
4 6 8 10 9 7 5 3 (paperback)
2 4 6 8 10 9 7 5 3 1 (hardcover)

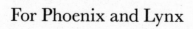

For Phoenix and Lynx

# Unicorn Princesses

## MOON'S DANCE

# Chapter One

In the top tower of Spiral Palace, Ernest, a wizard-lizard, leafed through a dusty book entitled *Formal Wear for Feathered Friends*. As he turned the pages with his scaly fingers, a bird with messy red feathers and bright green eyes grinned with excitement and hopped from one foot to the other.

Ernest looked up from a page that read,

"Magic Spells for Beginners: Wingtips for Woodpeckers and Spats for Sparrows." He furrowed his green brow and cleared his throat. "Bernadette," he said, "let me make sure I'm getting this right. You want me to turn one of your head feathers into a ball gown?"

"Exactly," Bernadette said. "Last year, I wore an emerald green tuxedo to the Starlight Ball. It matched my eyes perfectly. But this year I want to try a ball gown. I have so many feathers on the top of my head," she continued, looking up at her thick, messy head plumage and grinning sheepishly, "that I was thinking I could spare one to make the perfect dress."

Ernest nodded and flipped to a page

with the words, "Advanced Spells: Turning Feathers and Plumes into Gowns," in large, gold letters across the top. He read for several seconds and asked, "You don't happen to know what a plume is, do you?"

"It's just a fancy word for a feather," Bernadette said, shrugging.

"Then I think I've found just the right spell," Ernest said.

"Fantastic!" Bernadette said, twirling on one talon while she kicked the other foot in the air. "I've been practicing my dance moves all week."

Ernest laughed. "Me too! And I've almost perfected the spell for my tuxedo." He blushed and added, "It just needs a few, um, tweaks." He straightened his pointy hat and pulled his wand from his cloak pocket. "Are you ready for your ball gown?"

"Absolutely!" Bernadette said.

Ernest lifted his wand, pointed it at an unruly feather on Bernadette's head, and chanted, "Feathery Fancily Pleathery Plown! Turn this Ballroom into a Crown!" He stared expectantly at Bernadette. But instead of a gown appearing, thunder rumbled and a giant bolt of gold lightning tore across the sky.

"Oh dear," Ernest said, grimacing. "What did I do wrong this time?"

Bernadette peered over at the open page in Ernest's book. "Well," she said, pointing with her talon, "I'm pretty sure you read this line incorrectly."

"Oh dear! I sure did," Ernest said. "Let me try one more time." He studied the spell, mouthing the words silently. Then he looked again at Bernadette, pointed his wand at the same feather, and chanted, "Feathery Fancily Pleathery Plown! Turn this Small Plume into a Gown!"

Red light swirled around Bernadette, and suddenly she was wearing a scarlet ball gown with a sequined top and a gauzy skirt. "I love it!" Bernadette cried as she shimmied and sashayed across the room. "It's perfect for dancing. Thank you, Ernest!" And then she hopped out the door and twirled down the hall.

# Chapter Two

On a rainy Wednesday afternoon, Cressida Jenkins stood in the middle of her bedroom wearing a black leotard, pink tights, pink ballet slippers, and a turquoise tutu. She glanced at her bedroom door to triple check it was closed and locked. She didn't want Corey, her older brother, to walk in and see her practicing for her dance recital that weekend. If he did, he would never stop making fun of her tutu or the way she danced.

Cressida took a deep breath. She pressed the play button on her music player. And then, as she counted in her head, she leaped, spun, and twirled across her unicorn rug. At the end of her dance routine, as she prepared to curtsy, she heard a high, tinkling noise. At first she thought it was a part of the song she didn't remember. And then she realized the sound was coming from her bedside table drawer.

Cressida's heart skipped a beat and her eyes widened. She turned off her music player and bounded over to her bedside table. She opened the drawer and pulled

out an old-fashioned key with a crystal-ball handle that glowed bright pink. Cressida beamed with excitement. Her friends, the unicorn princesses, had given her the key so she could visit them in their secret world, the Rainbow Realm, any time: all she had to do was push the key into a hole in the base of a giant oak tree in the woods behind her house, and she would be magically transported to the unicorns' home, Spiral Palace. When the unicorns wanted to invite Cressida to join them for a special occasion, they made the key's handle turn bright pink—just the way it was glowing right then!

As quickly as she could, Cressida peeled off her leotard, tights, slippers, and tutu— the tights were too scratchy to wear all afternoon, and she didn't want to worry about tearing her tutu, which she would need for her recital, while she rode unicorns in the Rainbow Realm. She put on rainbow-striped leggings, a black T-shirt covered in gold stars, a green zip-up sweatshirt with a picture of a raccoon on the back, and silver unicorn sneakers. The sneakers were her favorite shoes: not only did they have pictures of unicorns on them, but they also had pink lights that blinked whenever she jumped, walked, or ran.

Cressida slipped the magic key into her sweatshirt pocket and skipped out of her room and down the hall toward the back door. She picked up the first umbrella she saw—an old black-and-yellow-striped one—and called out to her mother, "I'm going for a quick walk in the woods."

"Don't you want to wait until it stops raining?" her mother asked from the living room.

"I've got an umbrella," Cressida said. "And besides, I'm only going outside for a few minutes." Fortunately, time in the human world froze while Cressida was in the Rainbow Realm, meaning that even if she spent hours with the unicorns, her mother would think she had been gone only fifteen minutes.

"I suppose a little rain never hurt anyone," her mother said. "Have fun!"

Cressida hopped out the door, opened the umbrella, jogged across her soggy backyard, and found the trail that led through the woods to the oak tree with the magic keyhole. She couldn't wait to see her unicorn friends: yellow Princess Sunbeam, silver Princess Flash, green Princess Bloom, purple Princess Prism, blue Princess Breeze, black Princess Moon, and orange Princess Firefly.

When she got to the oak tree, she leaned her umbrella against the trunk so it would be waiting for her when she returned to the human world. She smiled for a moment at the feeling of the rain on her face and hands. And then she kneeled, pulled the key from her sweatshirt pocket, and pushed it into the tiny hole in the tree's base. The forest began to spin, until all she could see was a blur of blue, green, and brown. Then the forest turned pitch black, and Cressida felt as though she were tumbling through space. After several seconds, she landed on something soft.

At first, all Cressida could see was a swirl of silver, white, pink, and purple. But when the room stopped spinning, she found herself sitting on a pink velvet couch. Glittering chandeliers hung from the ceiling. Pink and purple curtains fluttered in the air. Cressida smiled. She knew exactly where she was—in the front hall of Spiral Palace, the unicorn princesses' sparkling white, horn-shaped home.

# Chapter Three

Across the room, a raccoon with lime-green stripes played a harp with his front paws and a drum with his tail as all seven unicorn princesses— wearing capes and glittering crowns that matched their magic gemstone necklaces— danced. Sunbeam twirled in a yellow sapphire crown and a gold cape dotted with sun-shaped sequins. Flash, wearing a diamond crown and a gauzy silver cape decorated with copper lightning bolts, did perfect pirouettes. Bloom, in an emerald crown and a mint-green cape with a glittery flower design, sashayed and pranced. Prism wore an amethyst crown and a purple taffeta cape with rainbow trim as she leaped and spun. Breeze, in an aquamarine crown and a blue cape embroidered with white swirls, and Firefly, in a citrine tiara and a shiny orange cape, swayed together to the beat. Moon, in an opal crown and a black silk cape with bronze stars, leaped and spun in circles as she swished her tail.

For a few seconds, Cressida smiled as she watched her friends. Then, she stood up

and sang out, "Hello there!" as she skipped toward them.

"My human girl is back!" Sunbeam called out, jumping straight up into the air and clicking her hooves together three times before she landed with a clatter on the marble floor.

"Welcome!" Flash said, rearing up.

"We're so happy to see you!" Bloom and Prism said as they shimmied toward Cressida.

"We're excited you could come," Breeze and Firefly said, grinning.

"Cressida! I'm thrilled you're here!" Moon exclaimed, racing over to Cressida and trotting in circles around her. "We were just practicing our dance moves for the Starlight Ball this afternoon. How did we look?"

"Amazing," Cressida said. She couldn't wait to hear more about the Starlight Ball. And she thought it was neat that, without even knowing it, she and the unicorns had been dancing that afternoon at exactly the same time.

Moon and her sisters blushed. "Well, thank you," Moon said, flicking strands of her silky black mane out of her eyes. The opals on her golden-yellow ribbon necklace and her crown twinkled. She turned to the raccoon, who had stopped playing music. "Cressida, this is Ringo. He and the other raccoons in my domain, the Night Forest, play traditional unicorn music every year for the ball. And this year, for the first time, the raccoons might even play some new music they wrote themselves."

"It's wonderful to meet you," Cressida said. "I love your music."

"Why, thank you," Ringo said, tucking the harp under his arm and wrapping his long, striped tail around the drum. "I'm sorry to dash off, but I have to head back to the Night Forest for a practice session with the other raccoons." He waved and scurried away carrying his instruments.

"I have a question for you," Moon said, twirling on her shiny black hooves. "How would you like to be the first human girl

to attend the Starlight Ball? It's a spectacular dance I host every year in the Night
Forest's very own ballroom."

"That sounds wonderful," Cressida said,
jumping with excitement. "I've always
wanted to go to a ball!"

"You've never been to a ball?" Flash and
Sunbeam asked, looking surprised.

Cressida shook her head.

"Not even one?" asked Firefly.

"Not even one!" Cressida said, amused.

"But if you've never been to a ball,
when do you wear your crown?" Bloom
blurted out.

Cressida giggled. "I don't have a crown,"
she said.

"You don't have a crown?" Flash,

Sunbeam, and Bloom said at once, eyes wide.

"Nope!" Cressida said, laughing even harder.

"The human world is such a strange place," Prism said, winking at Cressida.

"Now that I know you've never been to a ball, I'm even more excited you're here for the Starlight Ball," Moon gushed. "How would you like to come with me to help finish decorating the ballroom? Breeze and Firefly said they'd meet us there a little before the ball to help, too. If we go soon, we might even have time to listen to the raccoons' final practice session."

"I'd love that," Cressida said.

Just then, Ernest skipped into the room

wearing a glittery silver tuxedo, matching wingtips, and a sequined purple top hat.

"I've been practicing this tuxedo spell all week," Ernest announced with a wide grin. "How do I look?"

He spun around, and as he turned, Cressida noticed that instead of tails on

the back of Ernest's tuxedo coat, there hung two long, dark-green leaves.

Sunbeam, Bloom, and Prism looked at each other and smiled.

"I love your hat, but your tuxedo . . ." Flash began.

"You look ready to dance, except . . ." Moon started.

"What's wrong?" Ernest asked, his grin folding into a worried frown. "You don't like my tuxedo?"

"Your tuxedo looks great," Firefly said. "It's just that, well, I think something might have gone wrong with the back of your jacket."

Ernest blushed and grimaced. "Oh dear," he said. "Did I say 'mail' instead of 'tail' again? There are already stacks and stacks of envelopes all over my room."

"I think," Cressida said, recognizing the leaves from a vegetable dish her father often made for dinner, "you might have said 'kale.'"

"Oh dear!" Ernest said. "I'm so embarrassed."

"It's okay," Moon said. "You still have time to work on your tuxedo spell before the Starlight Ball. And if you can't get it right, there's nothing wrong with wearing leafy green vegetables on your coat."

"The worst-case scenario is you'll have an emergency snack on your jacket," Bloom added, winking at Ernest.

Ernest laughed. "I guess I'd better keep

practicing," he said. "But first, I want to make a ball gown for Cressida! I already made one without a glitch—well, almost without a glitch—for another friend this morning."

"Uh oh," Moon whispered to Cressida. "The next thing you know, you'll be wearing a spinach tutu!"

"I heard that!" Ernest said.

"I'd love a ball gown," Cressida said, jumping with excitement. "Do you think there's any chance you could make one with pockets? I like to have somewhere to put things."

"Of course!" Ernest said. He cleared his throat. He pulled his wand out from under his top hat. And he waved it at Cressida as he chanted, "Formally Normally Dancily Dockets! Make a Small Town with Two Big Rockets!"

Suddenly, at Cressida's feet there appeared a bustling miniature town, complete with roads, houses, train tracks, a hospital, a movie theater, and a school. In the center, right next to the school, were two rockets with bright red noses pointed toward the sky. Four tiny astronauts pushed a ladder against the side of one of the rockets, just below the door, and began to climb up. When Cressida bent over to examine the rockets more closely, she noticed little cars, trucks, and buses driving over the toes of her unicorn sneakers.

"Oh dear!" Ernest said. "Hold on! I can

do it right this time!" He held up his wand and chanted, "Snickety Snackety Snippety Snockets! Away with the Small Town and Two Large Rockets! Next Make a Ball Gown with Two Big Pockets!"

A bright pink light swirled around Cressida. She blinked and shut her eyes.

When she opened them, she looked down to see she was wearing a ball gown with a gold and pink sequined top and a gauzy pink skirt covered in gold glitter. Best of all, the gown had two enormous pink pockets. Cressida beamed. "I love it!" she said, and she plunged her hands into the pockets. Inside one, she felt her magic key. She smiled, glad to have it with her. Then, she spun and twirled in her new dress.

"What do you think?" Cressida asked.

"What a fabulous gown!" Moon exclaimed. "You look ready to go to a ball!"

"I knew I could do it!" Ernest said. "And now I'd better go work on a new tuxedo jacket."

"Before you go," Moon said, "I wonder if I could ask you for one more magical favor."

"Of course," Ernest said. "Anything at all."

Moon leaned over and whispered in Ernest's ear. He nodded as she spoke.

"Excellent idea," Ernest said. "I should have thought of that myself."

"Do you want to go check in one of your spell books before you try it?" Moon asked. "We most certainly don't mind waiting."

"No need," Ernest said. "I've got just the spell."

"But I really do think—" Moon began.

Before she could say another word, Ernest lifted his wand and chanted, "Darkily

Markily Mightily Sight! Please Make Cressida Glasses for Night!"

Wind swirled around Cressida. Suddenly, in her right hand, she held a pair of glasses with pink frames dotted with opals that matched Moon's gemstone.

For a moment, Ernest stared at the glasses. He blinked as his mouth hung open. And then he sang out, "I did it! I did it! I did it on the first try! That's never happened before!"

Cressida giggled and clapped. The unicorn princesses cheered. Ernest bowed several times. And then he tap-danced across the room and down the hall, singing, "I did it! And now to get this kale off my tuxedo!"

# Chapter Four

After Ernest disappeared down the hall, dancing and singing, Cressida looked again at her new glasses. "Should I put these on now?" she asked.

"Not yet," Moon said. "But I'm pretty sure you'll need them once we get to the Night Forest."

Cressida nodded and slid the glasses into her empty pocket. When she looked up, she noticed that Breeze and Firefly were frowning, whispering, and glancing at Moon.

"Is something wrong?" Moon asked. "If you don't have time to meet Cressida and me at the ballroom to help finish decorating, I completely understand."

"It's not that," Breeze said, looking worried.

"It's just that—" Firefly began. She sighed, furrowed her brow, and continued, "We heard you mention that Ringo and the other raccoons might play their new music at the ball."

"And we wanted to ask if we could stick to the traditional unicorn music," Breeze said.

"Why?" Moon asked, looking surprised.

"We don't know how to dance to the new music," Breeze explained. "And the one time I tried, I tripped and fell over."

Moon giggled. "That's because at the same time you were dancing you were also blindfolded and trying to break a piñata with your horn."

Breeze blushed. "Well, I guess that's true," she said. "But that doesn't change the fact that I don't know how to dance to it. And I'm afraid I'll look silly and feel awkward if I try again. The ball is supposed to be fun, and the new music will completely ruin it."

Firefly nodded. "I already have enough trouble dancing to the traditional unicorn music, and whenever I hear the new music, I freeze up," she said. "It will spoil everything."

Moon took a deep breath. "I don't know how to dance to the raccoons' new music either," she said, "but I think it would be fun to learn how. And it would make the raccoons so happy to get to play the songs they've written." She smiled hopefully at her sisters.

Breeze and Firefly looked at each other and whispered. Then they both shook their heads. "If the raccoons play the new music, we might have to leave early," Firefly said.

"Or we might not come at all," Breeze said.

"It will ruin the ball," they said at the same time.

"I just thought it might be fun to try something new," Moon said. Her hopeful smile bent into a disappointed frown. She looked like she might start crying.

Cressida put her arm around Moon's neck. She knew exactly how Moon felt: often, it was exciting to listen to new music or eat new food or read a new kind of book. But she also understood Breeze and Firefly's perspective: feeling uncomfortable was pretty miserable, especially at a dance.

"Maybe you need a little bit of time to think about what to do," Cressida said to Moon.

"Yes," Moon said, brightening. "I need some time to think about it." She closed her eyes and took a deep breath. Then she smiled, turned to Cressida, and asked, "Are you ready to help prepare for your very first ball?"

"Absolutely," Cressida said. Moon kneeled and Cressida climbed onto her back.

"We'll still plan on meeting you at the Night Forest ballroom an hour before the ball starts," Breeze said.

Firefly nodded. "Just please tell the

raccoons to stick to the traditional music," she added.

"I'll think about it," Moon said. "See you soon!" Then, with Cressida on her back, she galloped across the front hall of Spiral Palace and out the door.

As Cressida held onto Moon's silky black mane, the unicorn hopped along the clear stones that led away from the palace and into the surrounding forest. For a few seconds, Cressida turned and gazed back at Spiral Palace. She grinned as she spied a flash of silver and a sparkle of purple through the window of the palace's top tower. She bet Ernest was up there, perfecting his tuxedo spell.

"Thanks for suggesting I take a little more time to make a decision about the music," Moon said. "I think it would be so much fun to learn to dance to the raccoons' new music. The traditional unicorn music is fine, but, to be honest, I get bored dancing to the same songs over and over again."

"I love learning to dance to new music, too," Cressida said. One of her favorite things about her ballet class was that she learned to dance to music she had never heard before.

"Well," said Moon, taking a deep breath, "maybe if we get to the Night Forest in time to listen in on the raccoons' final practice session, you can let me know if you think it's possible to dance to their new music. And in the meantime, I can't wait to show you the Night Forest!"

# Chapter Five

With Cressida on her back, Moon turned right on a narrow path that wove through a grove of cherry and maple trees, and then galloped along a thick hedge covered in thorny vines with bright yellow, crescent-shaped flowers. She stopped in front of a hole in the hedge that was just a few inches taller than the tip of her horn. "This is the entrance to the Night Forest," she said. "Close your eyes!"

Cressida shut her eyes as Moon took several steps forward. Cressida heard crickets chirping and bull frogs croaking. Owls called out, "Hoo! Hoo!" In the distance, a wolf howled.

"Now you can look!" Moon said. Cressida opened her eyes. Above her, the moon, like a pale banana, hung amid more tiny silver stars than she had ever seen. In the light of the moon and stars, she could make out the shapes of a pond, a meadow, and what looked like it might be the edge of a dark forest. Even though she could see about as well as she could in her bedroom with her unicorn nightlight switched on, she had to admit she wished she had a flashlight.

"I can't see very well," Cressida said, gripping Moon's mane more tightly.

"I had a feeling humans can't see in the dark as well as unicorns," Moon said. "Try putting on the glasses Ernest made for you."

Cressida slid her hand into her pocket, pulled out her glasses, and put them on. Now she could see a pond with shimmering black water. Giant blue frogs with glowing orange eyes perched on the lily pads and croaked, their balloon throats bulging. On one side of the pond, a family of opossums lumbered through a meadow of thick, high grass. On the other side was a forest thick

with trees and vines. White and silver owls perched in the tree branches, their glowing yellow eyes winking at Cressida.

"Wow!" Cressida said. "The Night Forest is beautiful."

"I thought you'd like it," Moon said. "Can you see well enough to walk?"

"Yes," Cressida said. "These glasses are perfect. Thank you for thinking of them."

"No problem," Moon said, kneeling down as Cressida slid off her back. "Come this way."

Cressida and Moon followed a path carpeted in spongy green moss into the forest. Soon the mossy trail disappeared, and thick vines, tree roots, and rocks covered the forest floor. It was difficult not to stumble or trip, especially while wearing a ball gown.

Soon Cressida and Moon stepped into a grove of gnarled cedar trees growing among vines and roots so thick and knotted Cressida wasn't sure if she could keep walking without falling over. Moon paused, turned to Cressida, and smiled excitedly. "Want to see my favorite part of the Night Forest?" she asked.

"Absolutely," Cressida said. Then she looked up from the forest floor to notice hundreds and hundreds of gray stars, each about the size of a book, dangling from the tree branches.

"Do you mind if I make it so dark your special glasses won't work?" Moon asked.

"No problem," Cressida said. She wasn't usually afraid of the dark.

"I can't wait to show you Midnight Stars," Moon said. "Their magic only works when it's pitch black."

Moon pointed her horn toward the sky. The opal on her ribbon necklace twinkled. Sparkling light poured from her horn. Suddenly, it was so dark that Cressida couldn't even see her hands when she held them in front of her face. Though she wasn't afraid, she had to admit she felt a little nervous. She reached for Moon's back. When her fingers touched her friend's soft coat, she took a deep breath.

Just then, the stars on the trees began to glow. At first, their light was faint. But after a few seconds, they brightened and began to change color: from white to yellow to orange and, finally, to a vibrant red. Soon, the forest glowed a spectacular shade of scarlet.

"Wow!" Cressida said. "The Midnight Stars are beautiful."

"I thought you'd like them," said Moon. "And that's not all they can do." She cleared her throat and called out, "Midnight Stars, please take us to the raccoons!"

The stars began to wiggle, jiggle, and swing on the branches. Then they lifted off the trees, swirled in circles above Cressida and Moon's heads, and dropped to the forest floor in the shape of a long, glowing trail. "This way we don't have to walk on all those roots and vines," Moon said as she stepped onto the pathway of stars. They sparkled like rubies as her hooves touched them.

Cressida stepped onto the glowing pathway, and the stars shimmered. She took another step, and noticed that the stars

were quite smooth. They weren't slippery, like ice, but they were perfect for spinning and twirling, even in sneakers. Cressida turned and jumped as she walked, giggling.

Moon watched her and laughed, and then they both sashayed forward.

Soon Cressida and Moon were leaping and twirling together along a path of stars that led through groves of towering pine trees, beds of giant ferns, clusters of flowering vines, and marshes full of reeds and pussy willows. Then the trail of stars made a sharp right and ended in a sea of darkness that Cressida guessed was a meadow, though with all the stars' red light behind her, she couldn't see well enough to be sure.

"We'd better tidy up the Midnight Stars

before we go see the raccoons," Moon said. She shrugged and added, "Though I have to admit that I love it when it's pitch black." She pointed her horn to the sky. Her opal shimmered, and sparkling light poured from her horn. The Night Forest grew lighter, and immediately the stars began to wiggle and jiggle. Then they lifted into the air and flew in circles as they turned from bright red to orange to yellow to white and, finally, to a lightless gray. Then, like a school of fish, they bolted back into the woods.

"Thanks so much for showing me the Midnight Stars," Cressida said.

"My pleasure," Moon said. "Are you

ready to listen to the raccoons' practice session?"

"Yes," Cressida said. She turned to see that they were, in fact, standing in front of a meadow. And among the grass and wildflowers were the biggest oak trees Cressida had ever seen—they were much bigger than the one with the magic keyhole in the woods behind her house!

As Cressida and Moon walked into the meadow, Cressida noticed that spiral staircases, made of thousands of twigs fastened together with pine needles, wound around the trees and ended at oval-shaped doors midway up the trunks.

Moon paused in front of the biggest tree

and stepped onto the stairs. "The raccoons built these staircases just for me," Moon said. "Otherwise, it's not really possible to climb a tree if you have hooves. Want to come up?"

"Yes, please!" Cressida said, grinning. She had always, ever since she was a little girl, wanted to visit a raccoon in a hollow tree. Now she was going to get to do just that! She followed Moon up the stairs, holding up her ball gown.

At the top, with Cressida right behind her, Moon knocked on the door with her hoof. "Hello?" she called out. "It's me, Princess Moon."

"Princess Moon! Come on in," said a

voice from inside the tree. "Did you bring Cressida?"

"I sure did!" Moon said, nudging the door open with her nose. Then, she and Cressida walked inside.

The first thing Cressida noticed inside the hollow tree was that nearly everywhere she looked—hanging on the walls, lined up on shelves, even stacked on the floor—were musical instruments. Some looked like instruments she recognized from the human world: there were guitars, banjos, violins, flutes, clarinets, trumpets, trombones, saxophones, drums, xylophones, and triangles. But there were also instruments Cressida had never seen before, with curly pipes, strings at odd angles, many-sided drums, and spiraling keyboards.

In the center of the room four raccoons, each with lime-green stripes and mask, sat in a circle holding their instruments.

"Cressida, these are my good friends," Moon said, nodding toward the raccoons. "You've already met Ringo." He smiled and waved at Cressida. "And here are Renee, Roland, and Rita. In addition to playing traditional unicorn music on harps and drums, the Night Forest raccoons invent and build new instruments and write their own songs."

"Wow!" Cressida said. "It's wonderful to meet you. Thank you for letting me visit your hollow tree."

"The pleasure is ours," Ringo said.

"We've always wanted to meet a human girl," Renee explained, twitching her whiskers.

"We've heard the human world has wonderful music," Roland said. "I've wanted to visit, but I have a feeling someone might think a green raccoon listening to music was just a little odd."

Cressida giggled. "Probably," she said. "But you could all come listen to music with me in my room anytime! I wouldn't think that was odd at all."

"That would be fantastic!" Ringo said, grinning.

Rita stared for several seconds at Cressida's face. "Those are such wonderful glasses," she said. "You almost look like one of us!"

"Thank you," Cressida said. "They help me see in the dark."

"You can't see in the dark?" Renee and Roland said at once.

"I can't even imagine what that would be like," Rita said.

"Is it strange to need light to see?" Ringo asked.

"It's not strange to me," Cressida said, shrugging and smiling.

The raccoons nodded, fascinated.

Then Ringo said, "We were just practicing some new music we've been writing together. We're hoping Moon will let us play it at the ball. Would you like to hear it?"

"Absolutely!" Cressida said. "But first, will you tell me the names of your instruments?"

Ringo grinned. "This one," he said, nodding to an instrument that looked like a harp with four flutes poking out from the bottom and a drum on top, "is a flarpophone." He pointed to Renee's instrument, which looked like a large banjo with four blue keyboards wrapped around its body. "This is a quadruple-duple-banjinano." He laid a paw on Roland's instrument, which looked like five trumpets welded to the top of an accordion. "This is a trumpledumpledordion." He pointed to Rita's instrument, which looked like eight long, thin, curly saxophones arranged in a circle. It reminded

Cressida of an octopus. "And we just built this one today," Ringo said. "We're calling it an octogoloctohorn."

"Amazing!" Cressida said. "If you'd like to play your new music now, I'd love to hear it."

"Me too," Moon said.

Ringo, Rita, Roland, and Renee smiled and nodded at each other. Ringo tapped the side of his

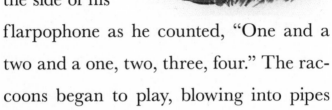

flarpophone as he counted, "One and a two and a one, two, three, four." The raccoons began to play, blowing into pipes and mouthpieces, strumming strings, crawling with their fingers up and down keyboards, and thumping on drums with their tails. The music sounded like a combination of the jazz her father listened to, the rock and roll her mother liked, and the show tunes her friends Daphne, Eleanor, and Gillian loved. The more she listened, the more she couldn't keep her toes from tapping. Soon her body was swaying, her feet were stepping, and her arms were waving.

She glanced over at Moon, who was swaying with the beat and furrowing her brow. "I really want to dance," she whispered, "but to be honest, I'm not sure how."

"Try doing this," Cressida said, stepping back and forth and waving her arms.

Moon took a step and then stopped. Her face looked uncertain.

"You can do it," Cressida whispered gently, twirling and kicking to the beat.

Moon slowly took another step and tried to swish her tail. And then she froze. "Maybe Breeze and Firefly are right and we should stick with the traditional unicorn music," Moon said, her face falling. "I want to dance to the new music. I really do. But I feel so worried about looking silly that I can't. Though I sure would hate to disappoint the raccoons by telling them not to play their new songs."

Cressida paused and thought about how to help her friend. She decided that the raccoons' new music wasn't the kind of music that you danced to by learning certain steps and sequences of dance moves, the way she did in her ballet class. Instead, it was the kind of music you danced to by making up your own ways of moving. "I don't think there's a right way or a wrong way to dance to this music," Cressida said. "Try closing your eyes and letting your body move in whatever way it wants to."

"But what if I look ridiculous?" Moon asked.

"Then we'll look ridiculous together," Cressida said, winking at Moon.

Moon smiled, even though she still looked nervous. She closed her eyes. For a few seconds she simply stepped back and forth. But soon, keeping her eyes tightly shut, she began to twirl, rear up, click her hooves together, and jump. For a moment, Cressida watched her friend. And then she closed her eyes too and began to spin and jump with the music. After a while, Cressida opened her eyes to discover Moon's eyes were open, too. The two looked at each other and began to dance together: twirling at the same time, nodding their heads to the beat, skipping and prancing around the inside of the hollow tree.

When the raccoons stopped playing their music, Moon and Cressida, both out of breath, burst out laughing.

"That was the most fun I've ever had dancing!" Moon said.

"Me too," Cressida said.

"Thank you!" the raccoons said, smiling proudly. Then all four stood up and took a bow.

Ringo cleared his throat. "Princess Moon, there is something we wanted to ask," he began. "Have you decided whether we can play our new music at the ball?"

"I'm still thinking about it," Moon said. "Breeze and Firefly really want us to stick to the traditional unicorn songs because they're worried they won't know how to dance to the new music." Moon smiled at Cressida. "But it's pretty clear there are all kinds of ways to dance to it."

Ringo, Rita, Roland, and Renee exchanged hopeful glances.

"I just need a little more time to make a decision," Moon said.

Ringo nodded. "Would you like us to play another new song?" he asked. "We could play a really fast one that's even better for dancing."

"Oh, thank you so much for offering," Moon said. "I'd love to keep dancing, but I think Cressida and I had better go finish decorating the ballroom. There are more balloons and more strings of glow-in-the-dark rainbows I want to put up. And Breeze and Firefly are going to meet us there soon to help out."

Cressida nodded. She wanted to stay and dance in the hollow tree for at least another hour or two, but she also felt excited to see the ballroom. "Thank you so very much for introducing me to your instruments and playing your new music for me," she said.

"Our pleasure!" Ringo, Roland, Rita, and Renee all said at once.

"See you at the Starlight Ball," Moon said.

And with that, Cressida followed Moon out the door and down the steps that spiraled around the tree trunk to the ground.

# Chapter Six

"I can't wait to show you the ballroom," Moon said as she stepped off the spiral staircase and into the grassy meadow. "The raccoons, wolves, owls, opossums, frogs, and I all designed and built it together out of rocks, tree branches, twigs, and pine cones."

Cressida followed Moon past more oak trees and through a jungle of tall, white diamond-shaped flowers. "The ballroom is just around this corner," Moon said as the path jutted sharply to the left.

As soon as they turned, Moon stopped short. "Oh no," she gasped.

"What's wrong?" Cressida asked, looking all around for the ballroom. All she could see was a clearing with a large, muddy circle littered with rocks.

"Something happened to the ballroom," Moon said, dipping a hoof in the mud and frowning.

"It was here?" Cressida asked, trying to imagine how a ballroom—even one made of rocks, tree branches, twigs, and pine cones—could just suddenly disappear.

"Yes," Moon said, her voice wavering.

"I bet it's another of Ernest's magical mis-haps. He means well, but he really is pretty terrible at magic." A tear slid down Moon's cheek. "Well, I guess we'll have to cancel the ball. We certainly can't dance in this mud."

"I'm so sorry the ballroom is gone," Cressida said, putting her arm around Moon. "But let's see if we can think of a way to still have the ball."

More tears slid down Moon's cheeks. "It took us months and months to build the ballroom," she said, her voice shaking. "I don't think we could possibly make another one in the next hour or two. I'm sure we'll have to cancel it."

"I'm not quite ready to give up," Cressida

said, smiling sympathetically at Moon. "I would be pretty disappointed not to get to go to my very first ball."

As Cressida tried to think of a way to save the Starlight Ball, she gazed out again at the circle of rocks and mud. And then she noticed something shiny right in the middle of where the ballroom had once been.

"What's that?" she asked, pointing to the shiny thing.

"I'm not sure," Moon said, sniffling. "Why don't we go see?"

Cressida pulled up the skirt of her ball gown as she walked toward the center of the circle, but she still managed to splatter mud all over her dress and her unicorn sneakers. She didn't mind. Life wouldn't be much fun if she spent all her time trying not to get dirty.

"I just polished my hooves this morning to get ready for the ball, and now they're getting all muddy," Moon said. "I guess it probably doesn't matter now."

In the center of the muddy, rocky circle where the ballroom had once been, Cressida crouched down to discover the shiny thing she and Moon had spotted: a crown made of thin gold wires, meant to look like vines, that twisted around bright pink, star-shaped sapphires. The sapphires, Cressida noticed, were exactly the same shade of pink as her ball gown. "It's beautiful," she said.

"It's gorgeous," Moon agreed, though her voice sounded sad. Then, with one of her muddy black hooves, she tried to move the crown. It wouldn't budge. Next, she tried to pick it up with her mouth. It still wouldn't move. "That's weird," Moon said. "Maybe it's stuck to a rock. Do you want to try?"

"Sure," Cressida said. She reached out and put her hands on the crown and pulled up, expecting she wouldn't be able to lift it. But to her surprise, it came right off the ground. As she held it in her hands, the crown began to glow and hum.

Moon gasped. "How on earth did you do that?" she asked.

"I don't know," Cressida said, feeling puzzled. "I just picked it up."

Moon tilted her head to the side. "How strange," she said. "Why don't you try putting it on?"

Cressida grinned and put the crown on her head. It felt light and comfortable, as though it belonged to her. For a moment, the humming noise got louder, and then a magic wand, made of a long, gold vine with a pink, star-shaped sapphire at the end, appeared in Cressida's hand.

"Wow!" Moon said, looking at

the crown and the wand. "Now you look like Princess Cressida. And not just Princess Cressida, but Magic Princess Cressida."

"You don't think this wand really is magic, do you?" Cressida asked, turning the wand over in her hand.

"It might be," Moon said, brightening. "Try waving it and see what happens."

"Okay," Cressida said, shrugging. She looked at a brown rock by her feet and waved her wand at it. She didn't expect anything to happen, but to her amazement, the star-shaped sapphire at the end sparkled, and light poured out. Then the rock disappeared and in its place grew a small, pink vine. Cressida giggled with delight and waved the wand at the vine again, this time holding the pink sapphire above the vine and lifting upward. The vine grew!

"I have magic powers!" Cressida sang out, jumping so that even more mud splattered all over her dress, her shoes, and Moon. Her unicorn friend smiled, but Cressida noticed her eyes looked even sadder and more disappointed than before.

"I'm so glad you have a new crown and a magic wand," Moon said, "but I have to confess I was hoping your special magic power would be to make a new ballroom appear."

Cressida put her arms around Moon and gave her a hug. "That would have been wonderful," Cressida agreed. And then, suddenly, she had an idea. "I think my new magic power might be the next best thing. I have a plan for how to build a new ballroom."

"Really?" Moon said, looking doubtful. "In just an hour?"

"Yes," Cressida said, looking at the pink vine for several seconds. "But we'll need some help from Breeze and Firefly."

"Well then, we're in luck," Moon said, smiling hopefully. "Look behind you."

Cressida turned around to see Breeze and Firefly galloping toward them.

# Chapter Seven

For several seconds, Breeze and Firefly stared at the circle of rocks and mud. Then Breeze asked, "Where's the ballroom?"

"What happened?" Firefly asked.

Moon told Breeze and Firefly the story of how they had come to finish decorating the ballroom, only to find a giant circle of mud and rocks. "But look what Cressida found in the middle of all the mud," Moon said, pointing her horn toward Cressida.

Breeze and Firefly noticed Cressida's crown and wand and grinned.

"I call her Magic Princess Cressida," Moon said. "Especially because she says she has a plan to save the Starlight Ball."

"If anyone can save the Starlight Ball, it's Magic Princess Cressida," Breeze said.

"Definitely," Firefly added.

Cressida blushed. "It's true that I have an idea," she said. "But I'll need your help."

"Of course," Breeze and Firefly said at once.

But then Breeze paused and looked at Moon. "Did you make a decision about the music?" she asked.

Moon grinned. "Yes," she said. "Cressida and I visited the raccoons during their practice session, and we had an amazing time dancing to their new music. It turns out it's even easier to dance to than the traditional unicorn music! I've decided that if Cressida can find a way to save the ball, I'm going to ask them to only play their new music. And then Cressida and I will teach everyone to dance to it."

Cressida felt surprised, but she had to admit she wasn't disappointed. The most fun she had ever had dancing had been in the hollow tree.

Firefly frowned.

Breeze sighed and shook her head. "Please, Moon," she said. "Let's not risk ruining the ball. Let's ask the raccoons to stick to the traditional music."

Firefly nodded. "I've been practicing my traditional unicorn dances all week. I don't want to spend the entire ball standing by the wall watching everyone else dance or feeling awkward and silly on the dance floor."

"But—" Moon began. She looked down at her hooves. "I really think we could all learn to dance to the new music together. It will be fun."

Breeze sighed and shook her head. "I don't really feel like helping to build a new ballroom knowing that I probably won't even want to stay at the ball."

"Me neither," Firefly said, frowning.

Suddenly, Moon, Breeze, and Firefly all looked like they might start crying.

Cressida took a deep breath. "I have an idea," she said. "I can completely understand that Breeze and Firefly want to have a great time at the ball, and that they're worried the wrong music will ruin it. And I can also see why Moon wants the raccoons to play the new music. She and I had a fantastic time dancing to it together just a few minutes ago." The unicorns all nodded. "So," Cressida continued, "why don't we compromise?"

"What does 'compromise' mean?" Firefly asked.

"Is that the name of the dance you made up to the new music?" Breeze asked, turning up her nose.

Cressida laughed. "'Compromise' means we make an agreement with each other where we all get some of the things we want, but not everything," she explained. "Instead of one of you getting your way, we could come up with a solution that takes all of you into consideration. My brother and I have to compromise all the time when we don't agree on what games we want to play."

"That sounds good," Moon said.

"Let's try it," Firefly said.

Breeze nodded.

"How about," Cressida said, "we ask the raccoons to alternate between old songs and new songs at the ball? That way, if there's a song one of you doesn't want to dance to, it won't be so bad because you know you'll like the next one."

Moon thought for a few seconds and said, "I'd be willing to do that."

Firefly shrugged and nodded. "I'd agree to that."

Breeze paused and sighed. "I guess that would be okay," she finally said, still sounding unsure. "But I'm still worried I'll have a miserable time. I'm not very good at dancing to the traditional unicorn music, and I've been doing that my whole life. I'd hate to have to sit out for half the ball if I just can't learn to dance to the new music."

Just as Cressida tried to think of another suggestion, Moon said, "I have an idea for another compromise." She turned to Breeze. "How about if you agree to try your hardest to dance to the new music?

And in exchange, I'll promise that if you try your hardest, and you still can't do it, I'll ask the raccoons to stick to the traditional music for the rest of the dance. What do you think?"

Breeze thought for a moment. And then she grinned and nodded. "Yes," she said. "I can agree to that."

Cressida smiled at her unicorn friends. "Do we have a plan that's okay with all of you?"

"Yes!" Moon, Breeze, and Firefly all said at once.

"Well done!" said Cressida. "It usually takes my brother Corey and me a lot longer to reach a compromise. I'm impressed."

The unicorns grinned.

Moon looked at Cressida. "Magic Princess Cressida, I think we're ready to build a brand new ballroom."

Cressida smiled and gripped her magic wand.

# Chapter Eight

Cressida walked to the edge of the circle of mud and rocks and waved her wand at the ground. The star-shaped sapphire at the end sparkled, and light poured out. Instantly, a thick, pink vine sprouted. This time, Cressida held the wand over the vine and lifted upward as far as she could, until the vine was nearly as tall as her mother. Then, still holding up the wand, Cressida took a step to her right. To her relief and delight, more vines instantly grew from the ground.

Cressida slowly walked around the edge of the muddy circle, growing a longer and longer circular wall of vines with each step. When she was only a few feet away from the place where she had begun, she made an arcing motion with her wand to form a doorway. Then Cressida stepped back and smiled at the pink, tangled vines that enclosed the new ballroom.

"Ta da!" Cressida said.

"I'm glad there's now at least a ballroom," Moon said, "but what about the floor? Do we have to dance in the mud?"

"I hope not," Cressida said, though she had to admit dancing in the mud might be at least a little bit fun. She looked at Breeze and asked, "Do you think you could send a giant gust of wind to bring all of Moon's Midnight Stars to the new ballroom?"

"Excellent idea!" Breeze said. The aquamarine on her ribbon necklace shimmered and blue glittery light shot out from her horn. Then a comet-shaped gust of wind appeared. It danced in circles above the wall of pink vines and then bolted away toward the thick part of the forest where the Midnight Stars lived. A few seconds later, a swirling cyclone of gray stars twisted toward them and entered the ballroom through the arched entrance. Inside, the wind turned into a blizzard that filled the air with stars. Then, with one final gust, they fluttered downward into a pile on the floor.

"I know what to do now!" Moon said, grinning. She pointed her horn toward the sky. Her opal shimmered as sparkling light poured from her horn. Suddenly,

everything went pitch black. After a few seconds, the stars began to glow again, brightening as they turned from white to yellow to orange to red.

"Midnight Stars, make a dance floor, please!" Moon called out.

The Midnight Stars lifted off the ground and swirled above the mud and rocks. Then, they dropped down to form a perfect red, glowing floor for the ballroom.

"Excellent work, Breeze and Moon," Cressida said.

When she turned to her unicorn friends she noticed that Breeze's gust of wind had left their tails and manes a frizzy, windblown mess. She reached up and touched her own hair. It felt like a bird's nest that was even more tangled than the vines that formed the ballroom's walls.

"I guess we're all going to have messy hair for the ball," Firefly said.

"We'll start a new fashion trend," Cressida said. "We can call it the Breezy Look!"

Breeze laughed. "It's special style that's just for dancing to the new music," she said, winking at Moon.

Cressida grinned. "Now I think we need just a little more light," she said, turning to Firefly. "Do you think you could create a swarm of fireflies that will hover above our new ballroom?"

"What a fantastic idea," Firefly said. She pointed her horn toward the ceiling. Her gemstone, an orange citrine, shimmered. Orange light shot from her horn. And then a cloud of fireflies appeared above the new ballroom so the inside glowed a warm yellowy red.

"I love it!" Moon said. "I think this new

ballroom is even better than the old one! Thank you, Magic Princess Cressida!"

"Yes, thank you," Breeze and Firefly said at once.

# Chapter Nine

Cressida slid her magic wand into one of her pockets and paused to admire their hard work. Just then Sunbeam, Flash, Bloom, and Prism arrived for the ball. For a moment, they stared in surprise at the new ballroom, with its pink vine walls, red star-tiled floor, and firefly ceiling. And then they smiled.

"I absolutely love the new ballroom,"

Prism said. "But what happened to the old one?"

"And what happened to your manes and tails?" Bloom asked, giggling.

"And why are you absolutely covered in mud?" Flash asked.

"And Cressida," Sunbeam said, rearing up with delight, "where did you get that crown?"

Moon and Cressida told Flash, Sunbeam, Bloom, and Prism the story of the missing ballroom, the magic crown and wand, the compromise, and the new ballroom. "We've given Cressida a new name," Breeze said. "Now we call her Magic Princess Cressida."

"Anytime you need someone to make

pink vines grow, you know who to ask," Cressida said, giggling.

"And," Firefly added, "we're calling our messy hair the Breezy Look. It's a special style that's just for dancing to the new music."

"Well, in that case," Sunbeam said, smiling playfully, "don't you think we all need to have the Breezy Look?"

Flash, Bloom, and Prism looked uncertain.

"I just spent hours getting my mane and tail ready for the ball," Flash said. But then she shrugged, smiled, and said, "Oh, why not?"

Bloom and Prism nodded.

"Four more Breezy Looks coming right up!" Breeze said. The aquamarine on her necklace twinkled, blue glittery light poured from her horn, and then a little blue gust of wind appeared. It swirled in circles around Sunbeam, Flash, Bloom, and Prism until their manes and tails looked even messier than Moon's, Breeze's, and Firefly's.

"How do I look?" Bloom asked. Her green mane was so tangled Cressida could hardly see her emerald crown.

"Absolutely breezy," Cressida said.

"Is that mud part of the style for dancing to the new music too?" Bloom asked, looking at Cressida's ball gown and sneakers and Moon's hooves, legs, and cape.

"Not really," Moon said.

Cressida shook her head. She didn't really mind the mud. But she supposed that if she were about to go to a ball, it might be nice to have a clean ball gown.

"Allow me to help," Bloom said. Her emerald glittered. She pointed her horn at a large mud stain on Cressida's gown. Glittery light shot out, and the spot of mud shrank until Cressida couldn't see it. Bloom kept shrinking the splattered mud until Cressida's ball gown looked as clean as it had when Ernest first made it. Then she shrank all the splatters of mud on Moon.

"Thank you!" Cressida and Moon said at the same time.

Just then, Cressida turned around and spotted Ringo, Renee, Roland, and Rita walking toward them. The raccoons, wearing their tuxedos, carried harps, drums, flarpophones, quadruple-duple-banjinanos, trumpledumpledordions, and octogolocto-horns. "We love the new ballroom!" Ringo said as he and his friends walked through the entrance and began to set up their instruments.

"I'm so excited, I can't stand it!" Moon said. "And I'd better go tell the raccoons about our music compromise." She galloped into the ballroom and then leaped and spun across the floor toward the raccoons. Cressida and the other unicorns followed her into the ballroom. The stars sparkled like rubies as Cressida stepped on them, and she spun and twirled on the new dance floor. It was absolutely perfect for dancing.

Suddenly, Ernest skipped into the ball-room in his tuxedo, which now had tails instead of kale. And right behind him filed in more different creatures than Cressida could count, all wearing tuxedos and ball gowns. There were dragons, foxes, rabbits, gnomes, elves, mini-dragons, fairies, cats, butterflies, wolves, turtles, and birds. Cressida even noticed a red bird with messy feathers in the brightest, reddest ball gown she could imagine.

Cressida heard Ringo counting out loud, just the way he had in the hollow tree, and then the raccoons began to play the song they had played for Moon and Cressida. At first, all the unicorn princesses except Moon froze, unsure of how to dance.

Moon trotted up to her sisters and said, "Magic Princess Cressida taught me that this is a kind of music that you can dance to in any way you want. There are no rules or steps or right ways or wrong ways. Just close your eyes and move in whatever way feels best."

Sunbeam and Prism grinned, closed their eyes, and immediately began to twirl, jump, and spin. Bloom and Flash watched for several seconds, shrugged, and shut their eyes. At first they just swayed to the beat, but soon they were doing what looked like a square dance. Breeze and Firefly stood stiffly, looking uncomfortable. Moon smiled reassuringly and said, "I think I felt exactly the same way you do now when I first tried to dance to this song. Just close your eyes and give it a try!"

"Do you promise not to laugh at us?" Breeze asked.

"Absolutely," Moon said. "I promise."

Breeze and Firefly closed their eyes. They shuffled back and forth for several seconds. And then they began to tap their hooves. "That's right," Cressida said encouragingly. She tapped her unicorn sneakers along with them.

Next, Breeze began to swish her tail and shake her head. And Firefly nodded with the beat and shuffled her front feet. "Excellent," Moon said.

And then, to Cressida's delight, Breeze and Firefly began to dance along with everyone else. Soon, Cressida, Flash, Sun-beam, Bloom, Prism, Breeze, and Firefly were leaping, kicking, spinning, swaying, shimmying, and twirling.

At the end of the song, Moon, breathless from dancing, exclaimed, "This is the best Starlight Ball we've ever had! Thank you, Magic Princess Cressida!"

"Yes," agreed Breeze and Firefly. "Thank you."

Before Cressida could respond, the rac-coons launched into a traditional unicorn song. Again, all the unicorns began to dance. The song reminded Cressida of the music for her dance recital that weekend, and she used some of the steps she had been practicing at home that afternoon.

Cressida and the unicorns danced to song after song, until Ringo announced, "This will be our last song!"

Cressida felt disappointed—she could have danced for at least two more hours—but she was also hungry and thirsty. As the band started to play one of their new songs, the unicorns rushed over to Cressida and formed a circle around her.

"Thank you so much for saving the Starlight Ball," Flash said.

"We're going to name this the Magic Princess Cressida Ballroom in honor of you," Moon said.

"I'm so glad I could help," Cressida said.

As the raccoons played the final notes

of the last song, Cressida said, "Thank you for inviting me to your ball. I've had a wonderful time, but I think I'd better return to the human world now."

"See you soon!" Moon said.

"We had so much fun dancing with you!" Sunbeam said.

"We can't wait for your next visit!" Flash said.

Bloom, Prism, and Breeze said, "Good-bye, Magic Princess Cressida!"

And Firefly nodded and winked.

Cressida pulled her key from her pocket. She wrapped both hands around the crystal-ball handle and closed her eyes. "Take me home, please," she said.

Immediately, the ballroom began to spin

into a pink blur, and then everything went pitch black. Cressida felt as though she were lifting off from the ground and soaring through the sky. And then she landed on something wet. At first, all she could see was a swirl of gray, green, and brown. But soon the woods stopped spinning, and she found herself sitting on the soggy ground, right beneath the giant oak tree.

Next to her, the yellow-and-black-striped umbrella leaned against the tree trunk. She was wearing her rainbow leggings, her T-shirt with the star design, her green raccoon sweatshirt, and her silver unicorn sneakers. She touched her head, hoping her crown might still somehow be there. She felt her hair, tangled from Breeze's gust of wind and all her enthusiastic dancing. Though the crown was gone, she felt something small and metal in her hair. She pulled it out to discover a gold barrette dotted with pink sapphires. Cressida grinned and put it back in her hair. She picked up and opened the umbrella. And then she skipped home as her unicorn sneakers blinked.

# DON'T MISS OUR NEXT MAGICAL ADVENTURE!

# TURN THE PAGE FOR A SNEAK PEEK . . .

In the top tower of Spiral Palace, Ernest, a wizard-lizard, sat at his desk. He adjusted his pointy purple hat. He straightened his cloak. And then he picked up a large black book with the title *Spells for Fruitmobiles: From Grape Go-Carts to Mango Motorcycles*. He flipped to the last page, where he found a spell that began, "Extremely Advanced (Only for

Very Experienced and Very Skilled Wizard-Lizards): Transforming Household Hooks into Plum Cars." Next to the spell was a picture of a grinning wizard-lizard speeding along in a six-wheeled sports car made out of three giant plums.

"Well," he said to himself, "Mother Lizard did always encourage me to challenge myself."

He studied the spell, whispering the words, "Vroomity Proomity Verity Prive! Make these Hooks into Plums that Drive!" over and over again. Then, he pulled a screwdriver from his desk drawer and marched across the room to where three spare wizard's cloaks hung on three gold hooks.

With his scaly green fingers, Ernest unscrewed the hooks from the wall, leaving the cloaks in a heap on the floor. He lined up the hooks on his desktop, glanced at the spell one last time, and pulled his wand from his cloak pocket. As he waved his wand above the hooks, he chanted, "Vroomity Proomity Verity Prive! Make Firefly's Books Come Alive!"

Ernest waited for a flash of light or a swirl of wind. He watched the hooks for any sign that they were turning purple or growing wheels. But instead, thunder rumbled in the distance and the palace lights flickered. Ernest nervously glanced out the window just in time to see three bolts of orange lightning tear across the sky.

"Oh dear! Oh dear!" Ernest said. "I've done it again!" He reread the spell and grimaced. "I must have been so excited for Firefly's new library that I said the wrong thing. Hopefully she won't notice anything amiss." He sighed. And then he smiled to himself and added, "But I still really do want to drive a plum car!"

He read through the spell again. He lifted his wand. He opened his mouth. But before he could say, "Vroomity," six more orange lightning bolts flashed and thunder boomed so loudly the hooks rattled against his desktop.

Ernest paused. He grimaced. "On second thought, maybe I'd better try something else," he said.

**Emily Bliss** lives just down the street from a forest. From her living room window, she can see a big oak tree with a magic keyhole. Like Cressida Jenkins, she knows that unicorns are real.

**Sydney Hanson** was raised in Minnesota alongside numerous pets and brothers. She has worked for several animation shops, including Nickelodeon and Disney Interactive. In her spare time she enjoys traveling and spending time outside with her adopted brother, a Labrador retriever named Cash. She lives in Los Angeles.

www.sydwiki.tumblr.com